I0763399

The United States Marine Corps

When the Korean War broke out in June 1950, there were no U.S. Marines on the Korean peninsula. This changed quickly, as elements of the Ist Marine Division arrived in August 1950. Marines landed at Inchon in September, 1950 helping to route the communist forces and push them northwards. During the remainder of the war the Marine Corps fought in such bloody engagements as the Chosin Reservoir, the Punchbowl, Bunker Hill, and the Nevada battles. The Marines gave the Communists everything they could handle and more!
Semper Fidelis!

DRAMATIS PERSONAE.
YANCEY.
GALLAGHER.
ROBINSON.
CAMP PENDLETON, CALIFORNIA. 1950.
ARE YOU CRAZY? THIS IS A ONE-WAY ROAD!
IT WAS TWO-WAY LAST TIME I WAS HERE...
THAT WAS FIVE YEARS AGO!
FALLEN HEROES
RICHARD C. MEYER, WRITER/ARTIST
ERIC WHITE, COLORS
TOM ORZECHOWSKI, LETTERS

McDERMOTT.
BROWN.
HUDNER.

TOO SKINNY... TOO FAT... TOO UGLY...
"TOO UGLY?!"
HEY! I GOTTA LOOK AT THIS GUY EVERY DAY FOR THE NEXT YEAR.

THAT ONE CAME RIGHT OFF A RECRUITING POSTER!
WHAT'S YOUR NAME, SON?
WOJITKIWIECZ, SIR!

I CAN'T SPELL THAT!
BUT... BUT... I'M A VERY STRONG RUNNER...

NOW THAT'S WHAT I'M LOOKING FOR!

WONSAN, KOREA.
YOU GUYS BEING RESERVISTS AND ALL, I KNOW YOU HAVEN'T GOTTEN PROPER TRAINING.
ALL YOU REALLY NEED TO KNOW IS "BASE OF FIRE" AND "FLANKING MOVEMENT."

SO IF WE GET ATTACKED FROM THE FRONT, WE'LL MOVE LIKE THIS--
WHO IS THAT ROCK SUPPOSED TO BE?
THAT'S NOT A PERSON. THAT'S THE OBJECTIVE.

WHICH ONE ARE YOU, SIR?
THIS ONE.
SO IS THAT OTHER BIG ONE THE ENEMY COMMANDER?
NO, THAT'S JUST A ROCK.
WHICH ROCK AM I?

YOU'RE THIS ONE!

LOOK, IT'S REAL SIMPLE. YOU GO WHERE I GO. YOU SHOOT WHERE I SHOOT.

WE FIND THE ENEMY OR THEY FIND US. THEN IT'S JUST STOMP, KICK, ANNIHILATE.
BASIC MARINE TACTICS.

ON YOUR FEET!
LISTEN UP! OUR MISSION IS TO PROVIDE CLOSE AIR SUPPORT FOR GROUND FORCES IN THE VICINITY OF THE CHOSIN RESERVOIR.
AFTER THE SUCCESSFUL CAMPAIGN IN THE SOUTH, GROUND FORCES ARE RETAKING TERRAIN ALL THE WAY UP TO THE YALU RIVER THAT BORDERS CHINA.
KOREA
WE CAN'T FLY AT NIGHT AND THE ENEMY KNOWS IT. THAT'S WHEN THEY ATTACK.
YOU ALL HAVE BEEN BRIEFED ABOUT THE REALITIES OF LIFE AS A POW. DON'T LET IT HAPPEN TO YOU.
DISMISSED.
JESSE, LET'S MAKE A PACT. IF I GO DOWN, DON'T LET ME GET CAPTURED ALIVE. DO WHATEVER YOU HAVE TO DO.
THAT'S A DEAL. SAME HERE.

SUDONG GORGE
HOW'S YOUR PLATOON COMING ALONG, YANCEY?
BETTER THAN EXPECTED.
YOU KNOW SOME OF THESE KIDS HAVEN'T EVEN BEEN TO BOOT CAMP YET?
I ASKED ONE WHEN HE WAS SCHEDULED TO GO AND HIS RESERVE UNIT TOLD HIM "NEXT SUMMER."
NEXT SUMMER... CAN YOU BELIEVE THAT?
HOW'S THAT KID YOU GOT FROM THE BRIG?
ROBINSON? HE'S A PRETTY ROUGH CHARACTER.
I WOULDN'T WANT HIM AS A NEIGHBOR, BUT IN A STRAIGHT-ON FIGHT HE'LL BE GOLDEN.
JUST KEEP YOUR HEAD DOWN, OK?
WHAT'S THAT SUPPOSED TO MEAN?
IT MEANS I KNOW YOU, JOHN. YOU'RE NOT AN ENLISTED MAN LIKE YOU WERE LAST TIME.
YOU CAN'T BE IN THE THICK OF IT ALL THE TIME. YOU GOTTA STEP BACK; KEEP SOME PERSPECTIVE.

IS THAT IT?
POOM
TATTATTAT
POOM
YEP, THE CHOSIN RESERVOIR.
YOU HEAR THAT?

PSSHT, "PERSPECTIVE". CAN'T SEE A THING FROM DOWN HERE...
FOLLOW ME!

TATTATTAT
TATTATTATTATTATTAT

SLOW DOWN, OLD MAN!
KEEP UP!
TATTAT
TATTATTAT
THEY'RE FALLING BACK!

KRAK

IS HE...?
I'VE GOT HIM. *GO.*
HE WAS JUST HERE AND NOW HE'S GONE...
NO TIME, GALLAGHER. MOVE!

TOOK YOUR TIME... YOU SEE THEM?
I CAN'T SEE THROUGH ALL THAT FOG.
THAT'S NOT FOG. THAT'S THEIR BREATH. THESE HILLS *CRAWL...*

GET DOWN! YOU'RE DRAWING FIRE!
I'M A LIEUTENANT. I'M *SUPPOSED* TO DRAW FIRE!
TAT TAT TAT
TAT TAT

POOM
I THINK WE MAY BE IN TROUBLE.
YOU THINK?!?
TIMES LIKE THIS, I FALL BACK ON THE OLD YANCEY FAMILY MOTTO: "EXPECT THE WORST--

"--BUT HOPE FOR A MIRACLE!"
GALLAGHER! WHAT TOOK YOU SO LONG?
WHAT DO YOU *THINK?* I'M CARRYING A 100-POUND GUN SYSTEM UP AN ICY HILL BY MYSELF UNDER FIRE!
SEE, ROBINSON? A *MIRACLE!*

WHY ARE WE THE ONLY ONES GOING AHEAD TO SEE IF IT'S SAFE?
BECAUSE WE'RE *EXPENDABLE.*
WHAT'S THAT MEAN?
IT MEANS THEY WON MISS US.

GRNNNRNN

WHAT DO WE DO? WHAT DO WE DO?
I DON'T...

TATTAT
TATTATTATTATTAT
OVER HERE!

YOU GOT A GRENADE?
YEAH, WHY?
FOLLOW MY LEAD!
TAT TAT TAT TAT
THAT PEA-SHOOTER WOULD BE USELESS ANYWAY.
TAT TAT TAT TAT TAT
HEY! OVER HERE!

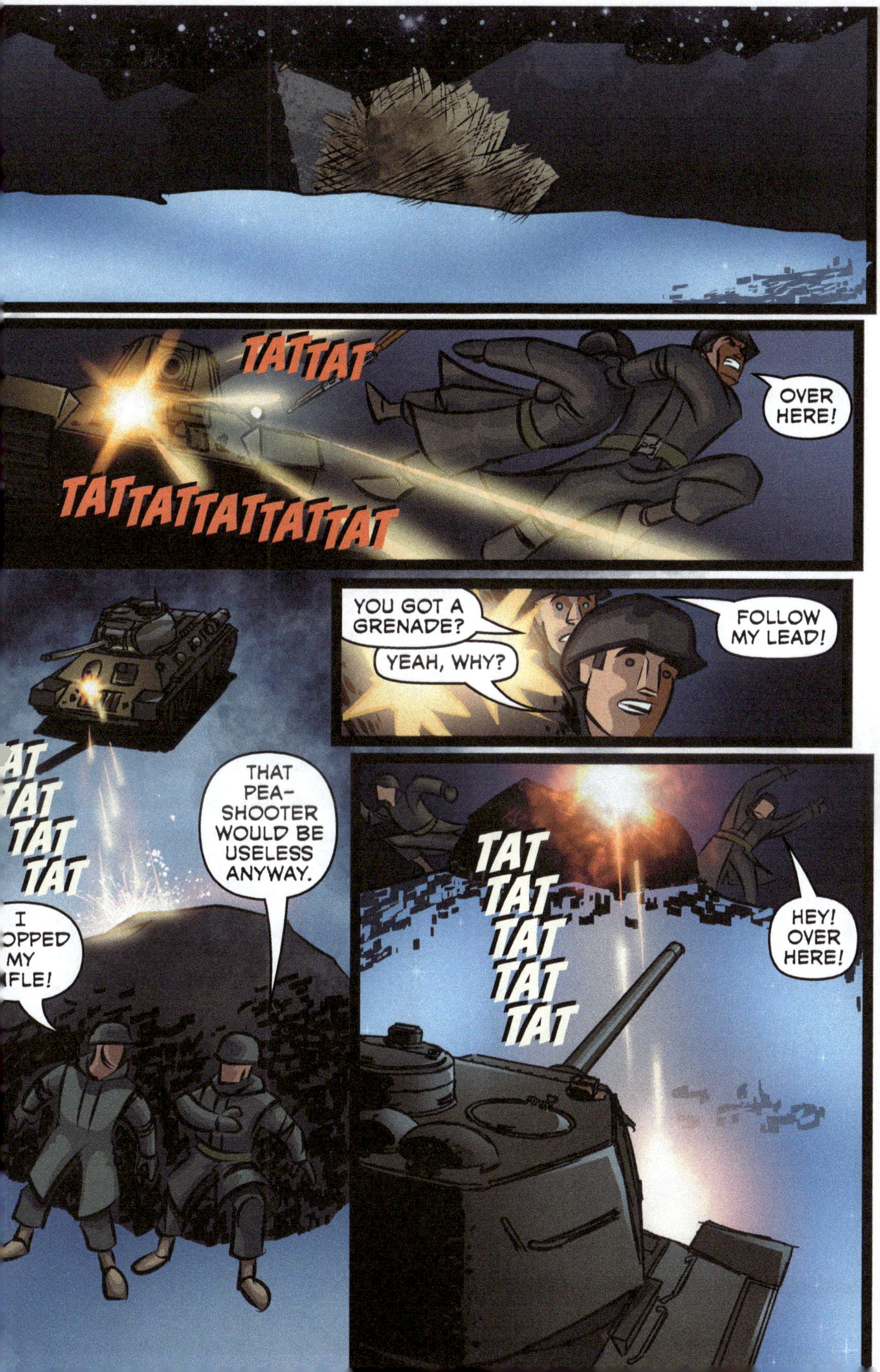

BOOM

RRNNNN

GRNNNN

KRAKK

FLIK
POOM
EXPENDABLE, HUH?

YUDAM-NI
TWENTY BELOW... CRANK OFF SOME ROUNDS TO KEEP THE GUN FROM FREEZING.
AYE, SIR.
BUDDA BUDDA
BUDDA BUDDA

WAKE EVERYONE UP! WE'RE UNDER ATTACK!

SOMEONE'S COMING!
QUIET! THEY'LL HEAR US!
DEAR GOD, PLEASE LET US LIVE THROUGH THE NIGHT...
WHAT ARE YOU DOING IN HERE?
THERE'S SHOOTING OUTSIDE. WE THOUGHT IT BEST TO--
WE NEED EVERY MAN OUT ON THE LINE.
WE'RE SUPPORT PERSONNEL, NOT SOLDIERS.

CHAPLAINS, COOKS. I'M A DOCTOR MYSELF...
I'VE NEVER EVEN FIRED THIS THING.
GIMME THAT.
YOU DIDN'T EVEN HAVE A ROUND IN THE CHAMBER.
NOW YOU DO.
THE PERIMETER IS COLLAPSING.THEY'RE BREACHING THROUGH WEAK POINTS. THAT'S YOU GUYS: THE "NOT SOLDIERS."
WHEN I THROW THIS FLARE, YOU SHOW THEM WHAT YOU'RE MADE OF.
FIRE!
BUDDA BUDDA BUDDA
BUDDA BUDDA
BLAM
BLAM

ROBINSON, GO SHORE UP THE RIGHT FLANK.
CLAYPOOL, HELP THE WOUNDED DOWN TO THE ROAD AND BRING BACK AMMO.
NNGG!!
HMMMM...
THEY'LL COUNTER-ATTACK SOON. THIS GROUND IS TOO HARD TO DIG INTO SO WE'RE GOING TO HAVE TO...

FINE!
YOU WANT TO SEE SOME-THING COOL?
...BUILD A WALL OUT OF THESE BODIES.
Y'ALL WANTED TO SEE THE FACE OF WAR, RIGHT? WELL NOW YOU KNOW-- IT'S ***UGLY!***
HERE THEY COME...

WHO'S IN CHARGE UP THERE?
THAT WOULD BE ME. YANCEY, JOHN. LIEUTENANT. ARKANSAS.
EXCESSIVE DETAILS ARE NOT REQUIRED. BASIC ARITHMETIC IS. COUNT MY MEN. COUNT YOURS. THEN DECIDE WHETHER TO SURRENDER OR NOT.
YOU'VE GOT AS MANY MEN AS WE'VE GOT BULLETS. I'D CALL THAT EVEN ODDS.
SO UNLESS YOU WANT A THIRD EYE-HOLE, YOU BEST TAKE YOUR LITTLE BAND OF MERRY MARAUDERS AND SHUFFLE ON BACK TO BEIJING.
HEEHEE, I LIK YOU. I'VE ALW BEEN FOND C ENTERTAINERS
SURREND NOW. OR DESTROY

WELL, YOU'RE DONE WITH THE EASY PART...
TALKING ABOUT IT!
BAM

INCOMING!

BAM
YOU OK, SIR?
ARGLEGARGLE...

AAARGH!
SHOOT ME STRAIGHT, DOC. AM I GOING TO LOSE MY TOES?
PROBABLY.
NICE BEDSIDE MANNER, JERK!
LOOK AT ME. I CAN'T TREAT PATIENTS WITH GIANT MITTENS ON. YOU'RE GOING TO LOSE YOUR TOES; I'M GOING TO LOSE MY FINGERS!
MAKE ROOM! MORE COMING IN!
WHO YOU WITH, KID?
EASY COMPANY.
HOW THEY DOING?
THEY'RE GETTING CHOPPED TO PIECES.
WELL, THAT'S IT. I'M NOT GOING TO STAY HERE JUST SO I CAN LOSE MY FINGERS TOO!
GRRRRRRR

HEY! THAT'S MY HELMET!
MINE NOW.
TAT
TATTAT TAT
AAARRGH!!
GO BACK TO THE AID TENT!
MAKE ME!
HA! WELCOME BACK. GO TAKE THE RIGHT FLANK.
TAT TAT
TATTATTAT

HERE THEY COME! AIMED SHOTS WIN WARS!
KSSHHH
AARGH!
HRRRR!!
STUPID, OLD...

BANG
AAAGHH!!!

NO!
GETAWAYFROMME
I'LLKILLYOU!!!
JOHN! JOHN!
IT'S ME!
CLEM?! THEY TOLD ME YOU WERE *DEAD!*
BULLET JUST BOUNCED BETWEEN MY SKULL AND MY HELMET.
LOOK AT YOU... YOU'RE FULL OF HOLES. GO DOWN TO THE *BAS* TENT.
I'M FINE.
I JUST WATCHED YOU PUSH YOUR OWN EYE-BALL BACK INTO ITS SOCKET. YOU'RE FAR FROM *"FINE."*
I'M THE HIGHEST RANKING OFFICER LEFT ALIVE AND I'M *ORDERING* YOU OFF THIS HILL.

CLEM, YOU CAN'T DO THIS TO ME. THEY ***NEED*** ME!

YOU DID YOUR PART. NOW IT'S THEIR TURN. THIS ISN'T OUR WAR. IT'S THEIRS. THEY CAN HANDLE IT.

JESSE BROWN AND THOMAS HUDNER

A TALE OF HEROISM

Aboard USS Leyte, Naval Task force 77 in the Sea of Japan - Dec 4th 1950. Lieutenant junior grade Jesse Brown, the navy's first African-American Aviator, and his squadron-mate Lieutenant Thomas Hudner launched off the carrier in their F4U Corsairs on an airstrike mission to support American forces encircled by the enemy at the Chosin Reservoir. During the mission, Brown's Corsair was hit by enemy fire and crashed. Lieutenant Hudner, seeing that lieutenant junior grade Brown was wounded and unable to get out of the cockpit, deliberately crash-landed his aircraft to come to Brown's aid. Unfortunately Hudner was not able to save him. Lieutenant junior grade Brown received the Distinguished Flying Cross posthumously. For his efforts to save his squadron-mate, Lieutenant Hudner received the Congressional Medal of Honor.

TALK ABOUT A TARGET RICH ENVIRONMENT. THERE'S *THOUSANDS* OF 'EM.
TAT TAT TAT
TAT TAT
I'M OUT.

THEY'VE BEEN HAMMERING OUR BOYS ON THE GROUND ALL NIGHT.
PAYBACK TIME.
SWING BACK FOR ANOTHER PASS WITH THE ROCKETS.
THEY'RE ENDLESS!
TATTAT
ME TOO. HEAD BACK TO THE SHIP TO REFUEL, REPAIR AND RE-ARM.

TATTAT

HERE THEY ARE. LET'S SWING OUT WIDE AND CATCH THEM BY SURPRISE.
GOT IT.
TATTATTATTATTATTATTATTATTATTATTATTATTAT

I'M HIT!
LOSING OIL PRESSURE...
30
20
40
MANIFOLD PRESSURE
10
50
70
I WON'T BE ABLE TO MAKE IT BACK TO SHIP.
KROOSH
KRAK
NO!

YOU'LL HAVE TO DO A BELLY LANDING.
DROP YOUR ORDNANCE AND FUEL TANKS OR YOU'LL *EXPLODE* ON CONTACT!
BROWN!
THIS IS COMMANDER CEVOLI. WHAT HAPPENED?
HE HIT SOMETHING-- *HARD.* HE'S NOT MOVING.
RETURN TO SHIP. WE'LL SEND A RESCUE CHOPPER FOR HIM.

HUDNER--
WHAT
HAPPENED?
YOU'RE
ALIVE!
ARE YOU
INJURED?
IMPACT
PUSHED THE
DASH BACK.
MY LEGS ARE
TRAPPED.
I'M
GOING
IN.
LIEUTENANT
HUDNER, IF
YOU DITCH THAT
PLANE I WILL
TAKE YOUR
WINGS!
TAKE
'EM!

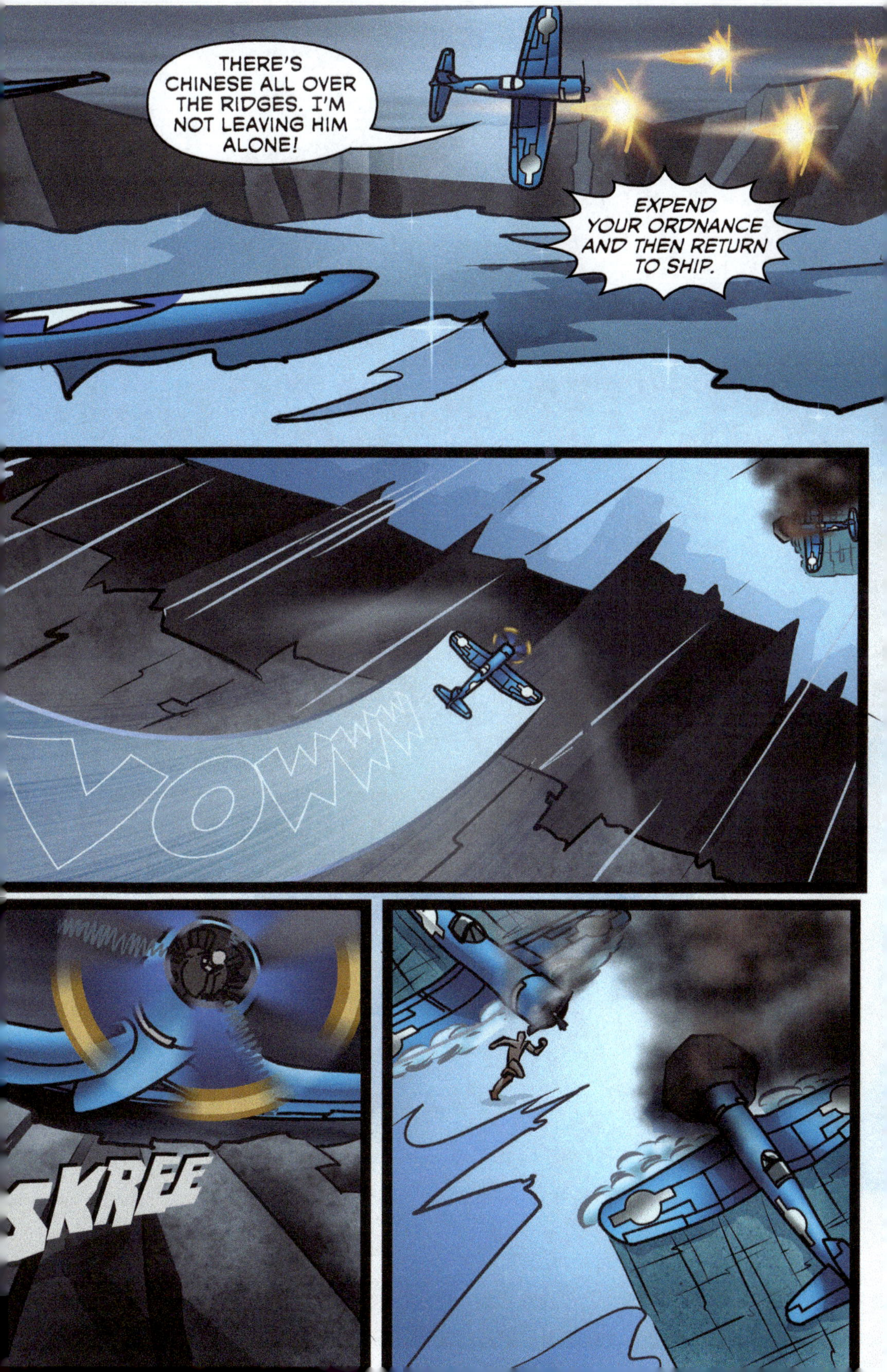

THERE'S CHINESE ALL OVER THE RIDGES. I'M NOT LEAVING HIM ALONE!

EXPEND YOUR ORDNANCE AND THEN RETURN TO SHIP.

VOWWW

W-WHY DO YOU DO THAT?
YOU ALWAYS KNOW WHY *YOU* DO THINGS?
STOP! ***STOP!***

SIT TIGHT. I'LL GET YOU OUT.
I KNOW IT HURTS. IT'S THE ONLY WAY.
CAN'T GET A GOOD ANGLE... SLIPPING...
TOM...STOP! YOU'RE KILLING ME!
IT'S OVER. YOU TRIED... IT'S OVER.
I'D LIKE YOU TO PASS THIS MESSAGE TO MY WIFE...
WHUP
WHUP
WHUP
WHUP

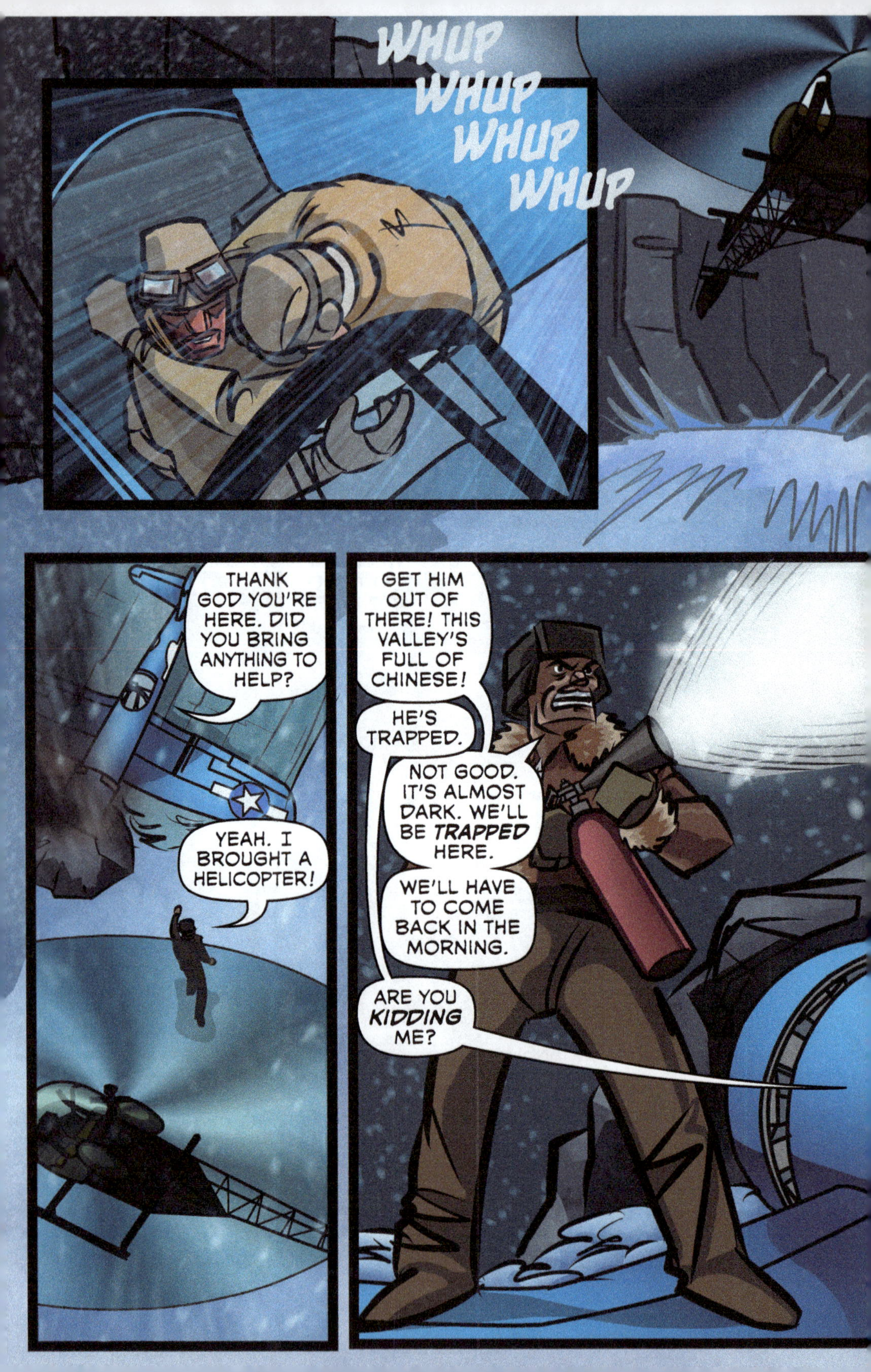

WHUP
WHUP
WHUP
WHUP

WHUP
WHUP
WHUP
WHUP

HE'S RIGHT. YOU'RE WRONG. GET ON THE BIRD NOW. THAT'S AN ORDER.

TO HELL WITH YOUR ORDERS! I PROMISED I WOULDN'T LEAVE YOU FOR THE ENEMY! I GAVE MY ***WORD!***

ONLY ONE OF US CAN KEEP THEIR WINGMAN OUT OF THE HANDS OF THE ENEMY AND THAT'S ME. GO. ***NOW.***

WHUP
WHUP
WHUP
WHUP
WHUP
WHUP

GET IN HERE!

HE'S WAVING GOOD-BYE.
I CAN'T LOOK. I CAN'T DO IT...
I CAN'T SAY GOOD-BYE.

GOOD-BYE.

LIEUTENANT HUDNER?
YOU HERE TO TAKE ME TO THE BRIG, SIR?

I CAME HERE TO SEE HOW YOU'RE FEELING.

HOW I'M *FEELING?* I'M WARM, WELL-FED; GONNA SLEEP IN A BED TONIGHT...
MEANWHILE MY WINGMAN'S DYING ALONE IN SUB-ZERO!

I COULDN'T LOOK AT HIM WHEN I LEFT. I JUST COULDN'T... WE MADE A PACT. WE WOULDN'T LEAVE EACH OTHER BEHIND. AND I DID.
IT WAS HIS CALL. YOU DID EVERY-THING YOU

NOT EVERY-THING.

I COULD HAVE STAYED.

THE CHINESE ARE ENGAGED WITH THE MARINES IN THOSE HILLS AS WE SPEAK. BUT AS SOON AS THEY GET A SPARE MOMENT, THEY'LL GET DOWN TO THE CRASH SITE AND PICK THAT PLANE AND OUR BROTHER CLEAN DOWN TO HIS BONES.
BECAUSE HE'S NOT A ***PERSON*** TO THEM-- HE'S A WAR TROPHY.
YOU MADE A PROMISE NOT TO LET HIM FALL INTO THE HANDS OF THE ENEMY AND YOU CAN STILL FULFILL THAT PROMISE. A FLIGHT'S GOING OUT AT DAYBREAK TO GIVE HIM A PROPER ***VIKING FUNERAL.***

GOOD-
BYE.
The END

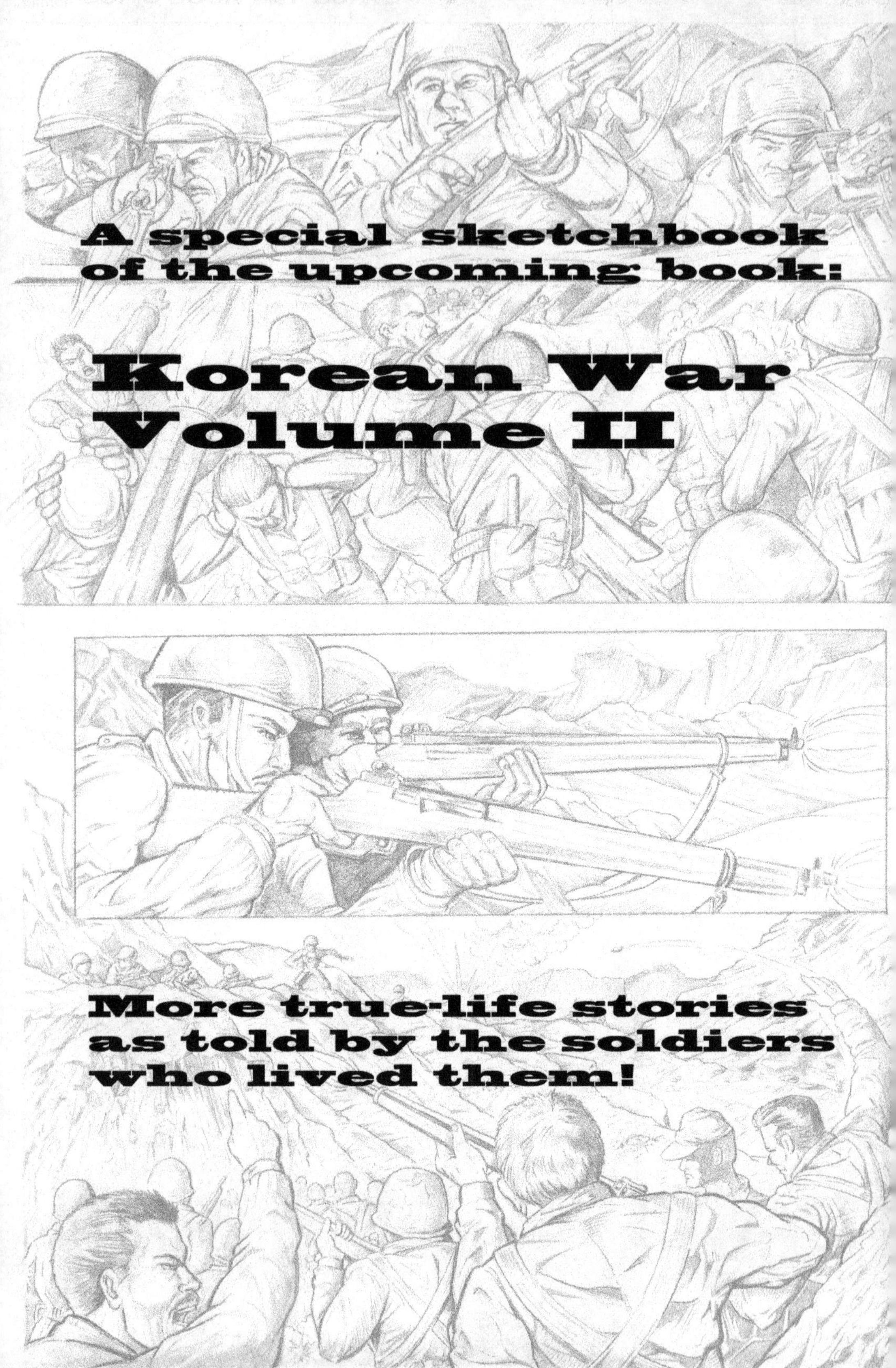
A special sketchbook of the upcoming book:
Korean War Volume II
More true-life stories as told by the soldiers who lived them!

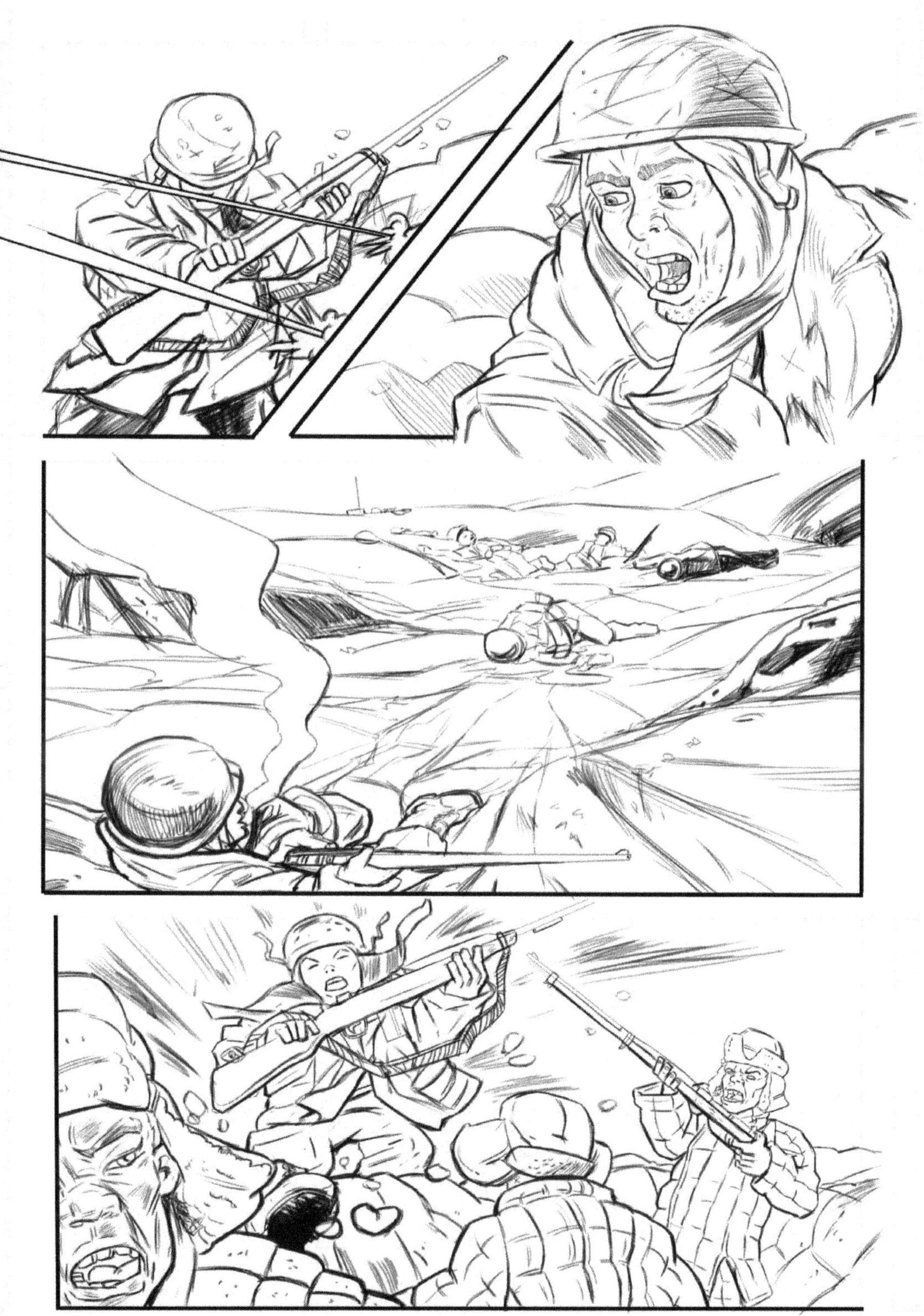

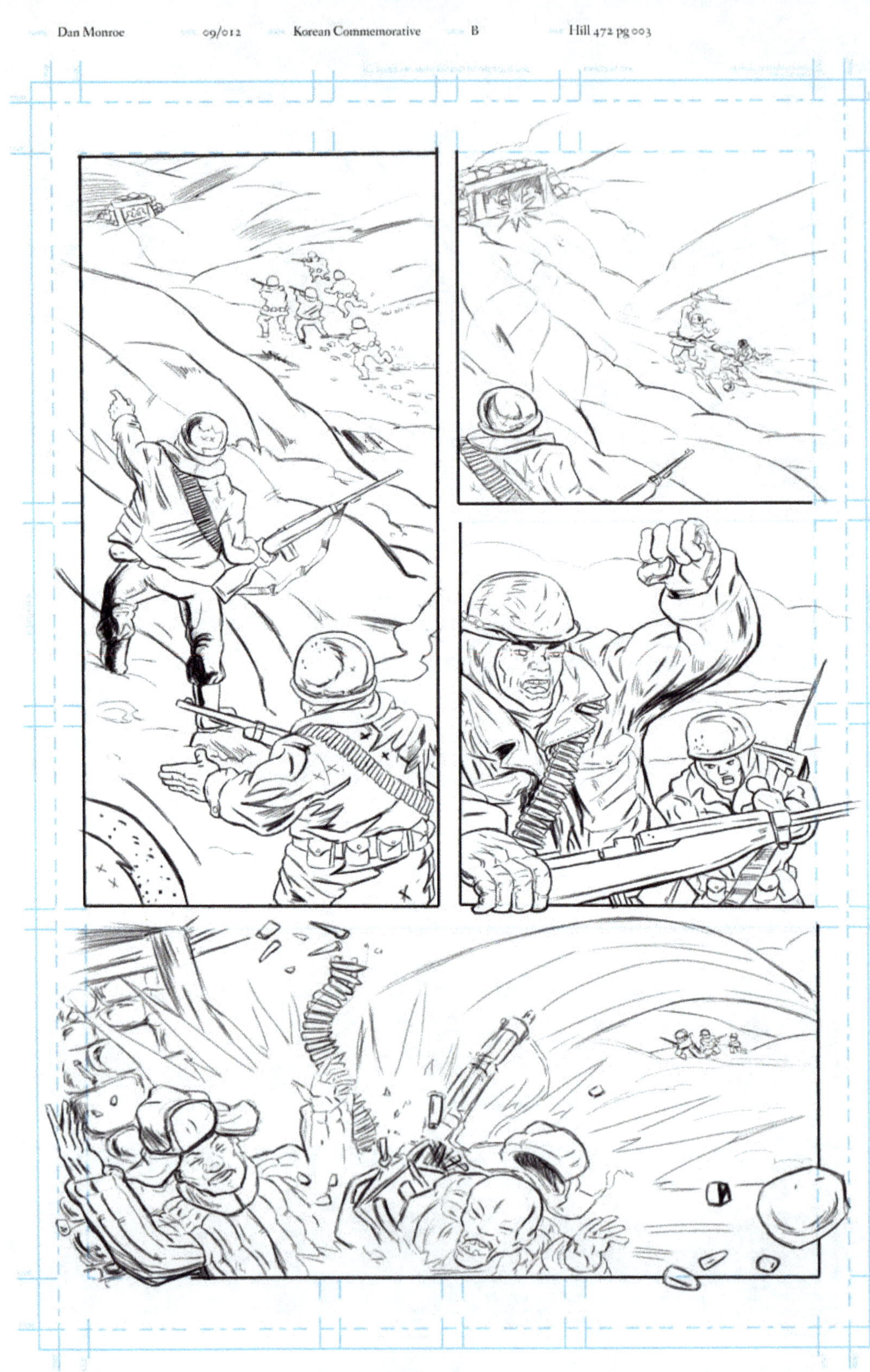

Dan Monroe 10/2012 Korean Commemorative B Mills 17 pg 002

US
US

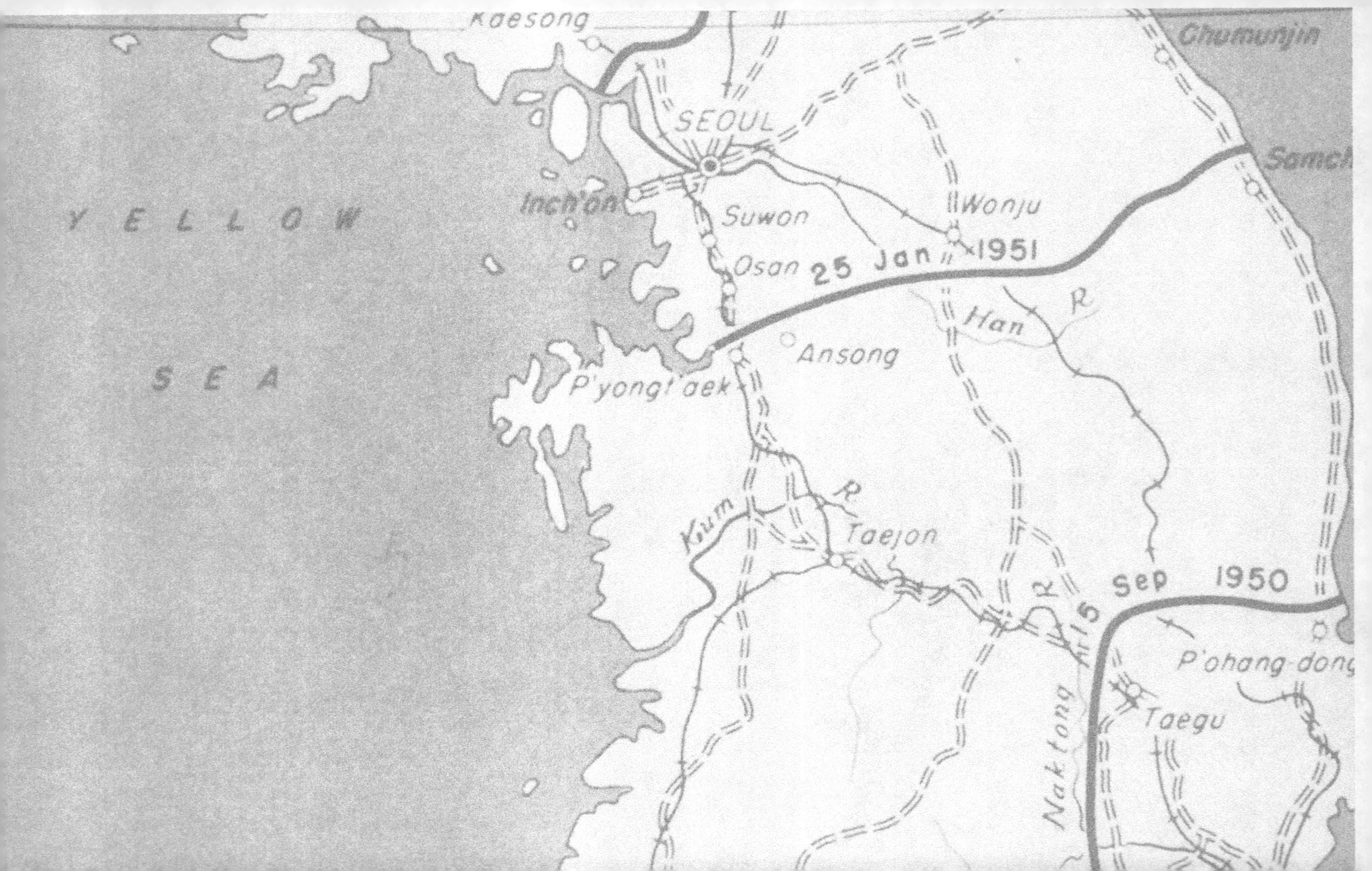
Chumunjin
SEOUL
Inch'on
Suwon
Wonju
Osan
25 Jan 1951
Han R
Ansong
P'yongt'aek
YELLOW
SEA
Kum R
Taejon
15 Sep 1950
P'ohang-dong
Taegu
Naktong R

THANK YOU FOR YOUR SERVICE AND SACRIFICE

FROM ALL INVOLVED IN THE KW60 PROJECT

HONORING ALL THAT SERVED IN THE

KOREAN WAR

Korean War Comemmorative Graphic Novel Volume 1 issue # 2 January 2013. First Printing. Created by Heroes Fallen Studios Inc.org

Printed in the USA

Digital proofs and production were done by Dan Monroe at www.dragonbrusher.com in conjunction with

Heroes Fallen Studios Inc.org at www.heroesfallenstudiosinc.org

www.ingramcontent.com/pod-product-compliance
Lightning Source LLC
Chambersburg PA
CBHW070620310726
48982CB00001B/131

9780983266716